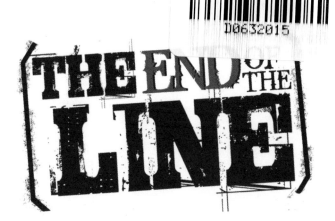

THE END OF THE LINE

BY GARY CREW

ILLUSTRATED BY GREGORY ROGERS

COVER ILLUSTRATION BY SERG SOULEIMAN

Librarian Reviewer
Marci Peschke
Librarian, Dallas Independent School District
MA Education Reading Specialist, Stephen F. Austin State University
Learning Resources Endorsement, Texas Women's University

Reading Consultant
Elizabeth Stedem
Educator/Consultant, Colorado Springs, CO
MA in Elementary Education, University of Denver, CO

STONE ARCH BOOKS
Minneapolis   San Diego

First published in the United States in 2008
by Stone Arch Books
151 Good Counsel Drive, P.O. Box 669
Mankato, Minnesota 56002
www.stonearchbooks.com

Text copyright © 1995 Gary Crew
Illustrations copyright © 1995 Gregory Rogers

First published in Australia in 1995 by Lothian Books
(now Hachette Livre Australia Pty Ltd)

Published in arrangement with Hachette Livre Australia.

Library of Congress Cataloging-in-Publication Data
Crew, Gary, 1947–
    The End of the Line / by Gary Crew; illustrated by Gregory
Rogers.
        p. cm. — (Shade Books)
        Summary: Overweight and shy, Janet keeps to herself at
school until Lola arrives and decides they will be friends, but Janet
is afraid Lola is just teasing her, as others do, when she reaches the
spot where they are to meet for a sleep over and weird things start
to happen.
        ISBN-13: 978-1-59889-859-0 (library binding)
        ISBN-10: 1-59889-859-0 (library binding)
        ISBN-13: 978-1-59889-915-3 (paperback)
        ISBN-10: 1-59889-915-5 (paperback)
        [1. Friendship—Fiction. 2. Overweight persons—Fiction.
3. Trolls—Fiction. 4. Horror stories.] I. Rogers, Gregory, ill.
II. Title.
PZ7.C867End 2008
[Fic]—dc22   2007003722

Art Director: Heather Kindseth
Graphic Designer: Kay Fraser

1 2 3 4 5 6 12 11 10 09 08 07

Printed in the United States of America

TABLE OF CONTENTS

CHAPTER 1

Half Moon Bridge

The bus rattled across a wooden bridge and turned off the road.

Janet looked up from her book.

Is this it? she wondered. She cupped her hands against the window to peer into the night.

The bus had stopped in a clearing that was surrounded by bushes and tall trees. Through the darkness, Janet could see the yellow glow of a telephone booth.

There it is, Janet thought. Just like Lola said it would be.

The driver turned off the engine and pushed his cap back from his forehead.

"Here we are," he called without turning. "End of the line."

Janet closed her book and glanced over her shoulder to the back of the bus. There were no other passengers.

She reached for the duffel bag at her feet. Then she pushed herself out of the seat. As she stood up, her book slipped from her lap and fell to the floor with a thud.

The driver had been watching in the mirror. "You all right?" he called.

Janet did not answer. She bent to pick up the book, then stood up and made her way up the aisle.

Even though she knew that the driver was looking at her, Janet did not look at the driver.

She felt herself turning red.

The little troll keychain that dangled from her bag clinked against the metal handrails of the empty seats.

When Janet reached the end of the aisle, she slung her bag over her shoulder, ready to step out.

The driver looked up and grinned. Janet wasn't sure she liked his smile. "I guess you'd like that opened?" he said, pointing toward the door.

Janet managed to make a small smile. "Well, yes," she said.

The driver folded his arms and shook his head, pretending to think it over. He said, "I'll open the door, but it's a dark night for a young girl like you to be out all alone."

Then, with a quickness that made Janet jump, a silver lever moved forward and the door burst open.

Janet stepped out into the night.

It was very dark.——

All around the bus stop, the bushes were thick and threatening. There was the phone booth, twenty feet away.

Janet turned up her collar, pulled the bag onto her shoulder, and reached into her pocket for the note Lola had written.

If you come, take the 403 bus to the Half Moon Bridge bus stop. I'll meet you at the phone booth at about 10 p.m. That's when I take Patch for a walk. You'll get to meet Patch, too. I hope you can make it.

Lola

Lola was the closest thing to a friend that Janet had ever had.

Usually people ignored her or were mean to her. Or they laughed at her, which was even worse.

Janet knew the bus driver had been laughing at her when she dropped her book, and when she walked up the bus aisle.

Janet knew exactly what she looked like. The girls at school called her Janet the Planet.

That all changed when Lola came to school.

CHAPTER 2

Lola

Kate Harvey, whose silver-blond hair fell in perfect waves to her waist, had been waiting in the office to get a lunch pass when Lola came to school for the first time.

Kate told the class that the new girl did not even arrive with a parent. She came by herself.

When Lola appeared in their class with the principal, she didn't look down at her feet nervously like the other new girls had.

Lola had stared straight at the class, deciding what she thought of them.

The rest of the girls hated Lola right away, but Janet was afraid of her.

Lola was a big girl too, but she wasn't overweight, like Janet was.

Lola was tall and powerful, with shoulders as wide as a football player. She had strange, golden eyes. She was not wearing a school uniform. She had on an old cotton dress.

In fact, as Kate Harvey told the class at recess, the dress looked like Lola had bought it at a thrift store.

Lola smelled, too. "She smells musty," Kate Harvey said, flicking her hair. "Like a dog. Like a stinking wet dog."

Janet listened from a distance.

Oh no, she thought. I hope Lola doesn't come talk to me! I hope she doesn't pick on me!

But Lola did talk to Janet.

The new girl noticed Janet right away.

By the end of the first day, whenever Janet looked up from her work, she saw Lola watching her.

She wasn't staring like the other girls did, with meanness in their eyes. Lola's staring was more like admiring. Her staring was almost as if she liked Janet.

On the second day that Lola was at school, one of the other girls accused Janet of cheating on the history quiz.

For punishment, their teacher made Janet stand at the front of the room.

Lola kept looking at Janet when everyone else went back to their work. Her look said, "Hey, Janet, I'm on your side."

Soon Janet held her head up and stopped sniffling.

Within a week, Lola was sitting with Janet at lunchtime every day. She would wander over and say, "Nobody sitting with you again?" or, "What's for lunch today?" or, "I heard what they were saying about you in history. It's not true that you cheat on every test, is it?" Then she would sit down with Janet.

Once Lola said, "When they call you Janet the Planet, just pretend it's because you look like a star. Don't think it's because you're fat."

Lola was sometimes mean and hurt her feelings, but Janet could not stop wondering about her.

What was it like to be so strong?

What was it like to be brave enough to never wear a school uniform and not care about getting into trouble?

What was it like to not care what anyone said about you?

Janet even wondered what it was like to have a name like Lola.

Imagine being named Lola and not Janet. Someone named Lola could be anyone she wanted!

When they were together, Janet always gave Lola some of her morning doughnut, or lunchtime sandwich, or after-school ice cream.

Lola never seemed to bring anything to eat.

It was worth it to share with her.

Lola stood up for Janet when she let her team down in the swimming meet.

"Forget about them," Lola said. "Come on, give me some of your cupcake."

Lola also took Janet's side when the Relief for African Orphans donations that the class had collected were missing. She said Janet couldn't have taken the money.

Janet felt awkward later when Lola produced a handful of change at Nicely's Milk Shake Stand and asked for a triple chocolate shake.

Janet felt worse when Mr. Nicely looked at the two girls and asked, "One straw or two, girls?"

Lola had answered quickly, without even looking at Janet, "One. My friend's on a diet."

At the end of the semester, Lola pulled Janet over to the far end of the school playground and handed her a gift.

"It's something special," Lola said. "A secret."

Janet was thrilled.

"I got it myself," Lola said. "I got it for you." She placed a tiny package of dirty wrapping paper in Janet's hand.

Janet's fingers shook as she opened it.

Could it be a necklace? Or a bracelet? A gold bracelet with Janet's name on it in pretty writing?

In her open palm lay a plastic and metal key ring shaped like a troll.

"Oh," Janet said, touching the troll's fluffy, dark blue hair. "It's very . . ."

"It's beautiful!" Lola said happily. "Just like me!"

Janet was afraid that the keychain had also been paid for from the money for the African Orphans.

"It must have been expensive," she said carefully.

Lola looked at her in amazement. Then she laughed.

"I didn't buy it," Lola said. "I took it. I went into the toy store and slipped it into my pocket. So it's really special. Do you see what I mean? Because of how risky it was to get it for you."

Janet nodded slowly.

She attached the troll thing to the zipper of the bag that she took to school every day.

She wasn't happy, but she kept it.

Lola was Janet's first friend ever, and keeping a stolen present seemed like a small price to pay to have a friend.

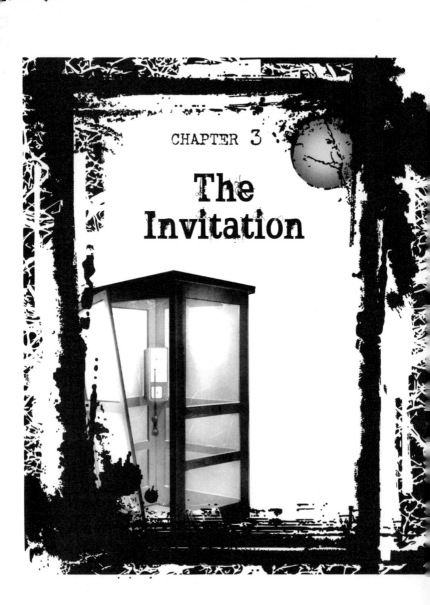

CHAPTER 3

The Invitation

Then Lola invited Janet to sleep over. Or, at least, she stuffed an invitation into Janet's hand one day at recess.

Janet read the note quickly. She could hardly believe it.

Then she took the note into the girl's bathroom, locked herself in a stall, and read it again. And again.

I want you to come and visit. You could sleep over. But don't tell the others. Secrets are always the best.

No girl had ever asked Janet to her house before, not even to watch a movie after school.

Now she'd been invited to sleep over at someone's house.

Like a pajama party. They would sit up until morning, talking and eating chocolates. Both of them in pajamas. Just like other girls.

Why not? Janet thought. Her parents were going to her aunt and uncle's.

Sleeping over at Lola's would be better than coffee and cookies and all that boring talk about all the other people in the family.

So Janet said, "Thank you, Lola. I would love to sleep over."

Now, here she was, right on time at the Half Moon Bridge bus stop. She had her duffel bag with her pajamas and favorite movies and magazines and chocolates.

But there was no sign of Lola.

There was just a phone booth in a clearing in the trees.

I'll go to the phone booth and wait, Janet thought. Lola will be here soon.

As Janet folded the note to slip it into her pocket, the engine of the bus roared into life.

She glanced back. The door was still open.

The driver leaned toward her and tipped his cap. "I'm leaving. The bus will be back at midnight, and that's the last trip on the schedule for tonight. Hope you're not still here then," he said.

The bus's door shut and the bus moved off onto the highway.

Janet watched it rattle across the bridge.

The light from the windows grew smaller and dimmer as the bus vanished into the night. Like a ship, Janet thought. She walked to the phone booth and put her bag in the puddle of pale light that spilled from the phone booth's door.

She stood and waited. No one came, not after five minutes, or ten. By the time fifteen minutes had passed, Janet felt nervous.

She was sure that her watch was right. It had said ten o'clock when the bus had dropped her off. Now it was 10:15.

She took Lola's note from her pocket and unfolded it.

She read aloud, "The 403 bus. Half Moon Bridge station. 10 p.m."

She looked again. The time was written right on a fold, and the paper had been handled and folded so many times.

Did it say ten? Yes. She was being silly. There was no mistake.

Janet turned the note over, holding it by the light to check. There was no phone number anywhere. For the first time she realized that she couldn't call Lola even if she wanted to. In all the excitement, she hadn't even thought anything could go wrong. She had been sure Lola would be there, like friends are supposed to be.

If no one came, if she was left alone, she couldn't call her parents. It was her first time sleeping over at a friend's house. She would never be allowed out again.

So she would wait. Lola would come.

Lola had said she would, because she was Janet's friend.

Janet moved her bag to the entrance of the phone booth and sat down, leaning back against the door.

When she looked up, the ring of trees seemed closer. The night seemed darker. She shuddered.

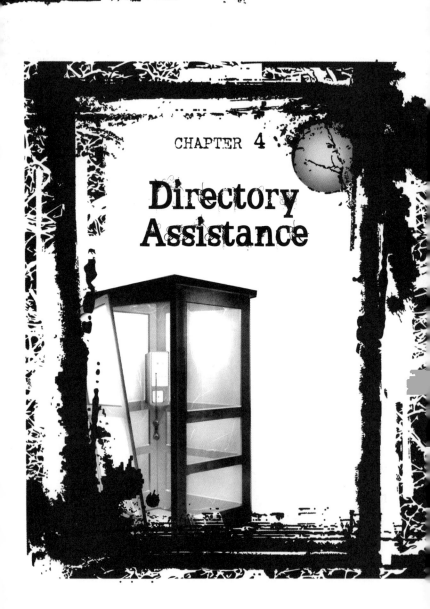

CHAPTER 4

Directory Assistance

At ten thirty, Janet couldn't wait any longer.

I'll call information, she thought. They'll have Lola's number.

She got up and opened the door of the booth. She stood on tiptoe to read the faded list of numbers printed above the telephone.

"Directory Assistance," she read aloud. "411."

She raised her right hand to dial and with her left she reached for the phone's receiver.

Nothing.

Her left hand grasped air. The phone's receiver was not in its cradle.

She looked down. The phone dangled loose. Its cord stretched almost to the floor.

Janet grabbed the phone and put it to her ear. No dial tone. She jiggled the handle. No sound at all.

"What?" she said. She couldn't believe it. She hung up the phone and picked it up again, listening.

Nothing.

She repeated the process, this time jamming the earpiece down.

She lifted it again.

Nothing.

She replaced it carefully.

"Please," she whispered. "Please."

Then, carefully, very slowly, she lifted the phone and listened again.

The line was dead.

She let the phone fall. Then she covered her eyes with her hands.

"No," she pleaded. "Don't let this happen."

Janet wished she had a cell phone like other girls in her class, but her family could't afford it. She was always having to use phone booths or call from phones in stores.

She lifted her head, trying to calm herself. She saw emergency numbers on the wall in front of her.

Muttering to herself, Janet reached down and grabbed the cord swinging beside her. She replaced the phone, then lifted it again, and dialed 911.

She waited, listening.

Nothing.

She hung up and dialed again.

This time she said the number carefully. Her voice was very firm. She spoke as she dialed. "9 . . . 1 . . . 1."

But there was nothing.

She was listening to silence.

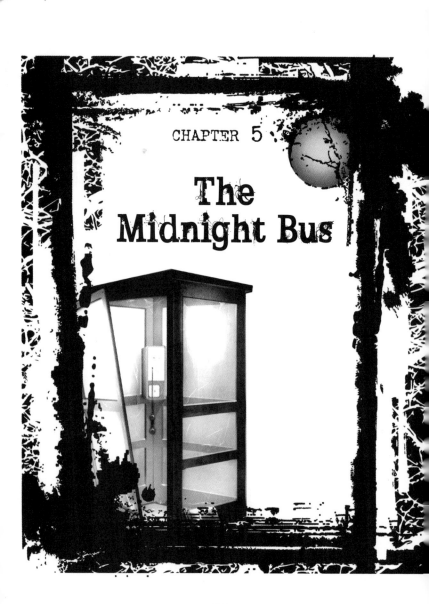

CHAPTER 5

The Midnight Bus

"It will be all right," Janet said to herself.

She replaced the phone gently and turned to the door. She was startled by the sight of her own reflection staring at her from the glass. She was shocked by the fear in her eyes, her worried mouth, and the paleness of her skin.

Janet moaned and opened the door.

A path of light spilled out at her feet, toward the darkness. She lifted her head, looking across the clearing toward the road.

There were no street lights, not out here. She couldn't see much, except for the outline of the trees beyond the clearing.

To her right was the shadow of the bridge.

It looks like a monster, she thought.

The bridge curved like the spine of a beast. Quickly, Janet turned away.

To her left the trees seemed thicker and the night seemed blacker.

She could not see the road at all.

"No wonder it's the end of the bus line," she mumbled. "It's the end of the road."

There weren't any houses that Janet could see. Not even far away in the distance.

She crossed the clearing and walked to the edge of the highway. She looked left and right again. If she went left, the road stopped at the trees.

Janet turned right and walked to the center of the road. She followed the white line until it stopped where the wooden bridge began. The metal bolts that held the boards gleamed like silver.

Janet stepped onto the bridge and felt the old boards shake beneath her.

The bolts that pin the boards down must be loose, she thought.

She stood still, listening to the silence.

"Don't be stupid," she said aloud. "You're freaking yourself out."

She forced a laugh and kept walking. The sound of the boards against the bolts followed her. Clink. Clink. Clink.

When she reached the top of the bridge's curve, Janet paused to look around.

Where does Lola live? she wondered. There wasn't a building anywhere nearby.

Then another thought crossed her mind. What if the whole thing was a joke? What if Lola was playing a joke on her? What if Lola was just out to get her, just like all the others?

Janet shook her head to try to get rid of the horrible thought.

She stopped and looked over the railing. Beneath the bridge was a pool of darkness.

Janet could not even guess how far the drop was, or what was beneath it. It might be a stream or a bottomless hole.

As she stretched her neck, looking down, Janet shuddered and pulled back from the rail to look around.

Someone's watching, she thought.

But there was nobody, nothing, except for the phone booth, its distant light warm and inviting.

"This is stupid," she said. She stamped her foot on the bridge so hard that the whole bridge shook.

"I'll try the phone again," she said to herself. "If it's dead, I'll take the midnight bus home."

Janet walked quickly toward the clearing where the phone booth stood.

At the phone booth she looked up the number to call for service problems.

Then she dialed again. Silence.

Well then, she thought, if that's the way it is, I'll just sit here and wait.

Janet looked at her watch. It was almost eleven. It would be an hour until the last bus came. "Yes," she said, "that is what I will do."

She stepped outside the phone booth and picked up her duffel bag.

Back inside the phone booth, she slid to the floor.

She put the bag on her knee to open it. But when she reached for the troll on the zipper, it was gone. Only the silver key ring was still there.

She went outside. Beyond the light from the phone booth, Janet couldn't see anything. She went back into the phone booth.

Janet dug in the bag for her book.

She needed something to pass the time while she waited for the midnight bus.

"I'll come and look for that troll in the morning," she said, adding, "if Lola ever gets here."

She looked up to check the position of the light on the ceiling and leaned forward so that her book was well lit.

Then, with one more glance at her reflection and a sigh of sadness, she opened her book and began to read.

In minutes, a group of tiny moths was fluttering around her face. Some got stuck in her hair. Some flopped around in circles on the open pages of her book.

"Go away," Janet whispered as she brushed them off. "Go. Get out of here!"

Then a black beetle flew through the crack below the door and hit itself against her face.

Janet was not so gentle with the beetle. She raised her book and swatted the insect.

The beetle hit the glass with a smack and fell to the floor on its back, hissing.

"Serves you right," Janet said.

As she settled down to read again, she caught a sudden movement outside the dark glass.

Janet froze, staring at the panels of glass.

All she could see was her own reflection. Her knees were pulled up, and her hands were gripping the pages of the book in her lap. Her pale hair hung forward, draped around her face.

All she could see in the glass panels was herself. But she knew there was something out there.

Something was circling the phone booth.

It was something that was smart enough to stay outside her vision, where Janet couldn't see it.

Whatever it was, it was moving beyond the edge of the light that spilled from her shelter in the booth.

CHAPTER 6

Patch

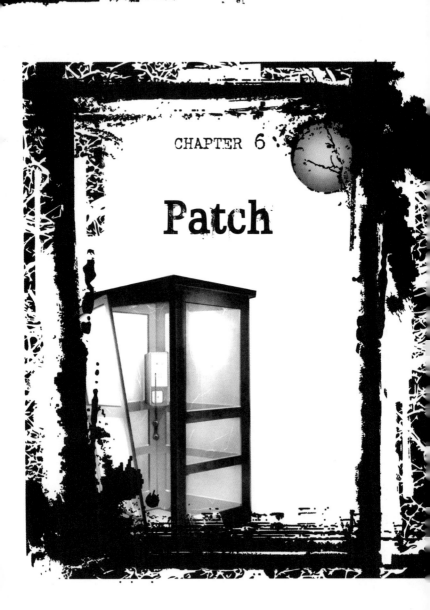

Is it human or animal? she wondered.

Janet didn't dare to cup her hands against the glass to see. She also couldn't trust her legs to stand so that she could throw open the door.

If she could, she would have shouted, "Get away! Leave me alone, whatever you are!" But she couldn't. So she sat, her eyes wide with fear, her ears waiting for the slightest sound.

Then it came.

First, it was some kind of sniffing, like someone gasping for air. Then it was softer, small padding sounds.

It sounded like gentle footsteps on a carpeted floor.

It didn't sound human. The footsteps sounded longer, like a dog.

And just as Janet realized what the thing was, there it was, its wet nose pressed against the glass.

Its pink tongue stuck out, and its floppy jaw slobbered on the glass. Around one of its golden eyes was a patch of black.

"Patch?" Janet called. "Are you Patch?"

Once, twice, three times the dog raised a paw and placed it against the glass.

Janet saw the pink and velvety pads on the dog's paw and its small claws.

"You're just a puppy," she said.

She looked at the dog. "Who taught you to shake hands?" Janet asked. "Was it Lola? Is Lola there? Is she?"

She reached out to place her own hand flat against the glass to match the dog's front paw.

At once the dog jumped up on its hind legs. Its front paws reached up on the glass. Its smooth, pink belly was exposed, and its long thin tail waved from side to side.

"If you're just a puppy, I shouldn't be scared of you, should I?" Janet asked the dog.

As if it was answering, the animal suddenly dropped down, ran around to the door, and thrust its nose under. It pawed at the edge of the concrete floor.

"All right," Janet said. "I'm coming."

She pushed herself up and the book fell to the floor, forgotten. Grabbing her bag, she opened the door and stepped out.

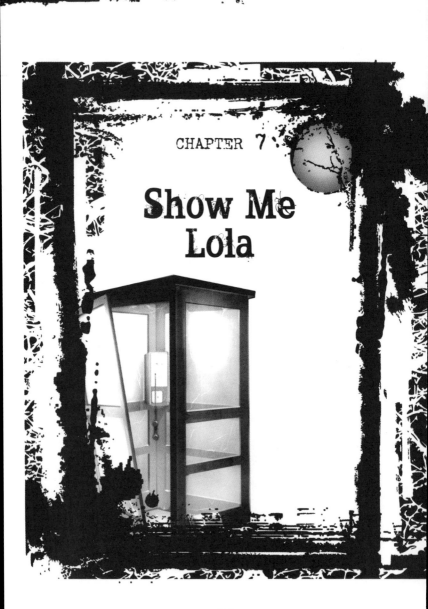

CHAPTER 7

Show Me
Lola

There was nothing.

No dog.

No Lola.

Only darkness.

"Lola?" Janet called. "Lola?"

Nothing.

"Patch? Patchy?" Janet whistled for the dog to come to her.

Suddenly the animal bounded toward her from the direction of the bridge.

Patch rolled on its back at her feet, offering its stomach to be patted.

When the dog jumped up again to invite Janet into playing more games, Janet looked around.

There was still no sign of Lola.

Janet put her hands on her hips and shook her head at the puppy.

"So," Janet said, "where is Lola? Where is she? Huh?"

Right away, the animal began to growl in a low voice. Then it dug in the dirt with its front legs.

Janet leaned down, curious. "Are you telling me something? Is that it? Lola? Is it Lola?"

As if in answer, the dog bounced away, bounded back, then ran away again.

Its head nodded, and its tail wagged from side to side.

"Where is she? Patch, where's Lola? Show me. Where's Lola?" Janet said.

This time there could be no doubt.

The dog turned away completely, taking three or four leaps toward the bridge, then waited, its tail wagging, until Janet followed.

"Go on," she said, waving it forward with both hands. "Go on. Where is she? Where's Lola? Show me, go on."

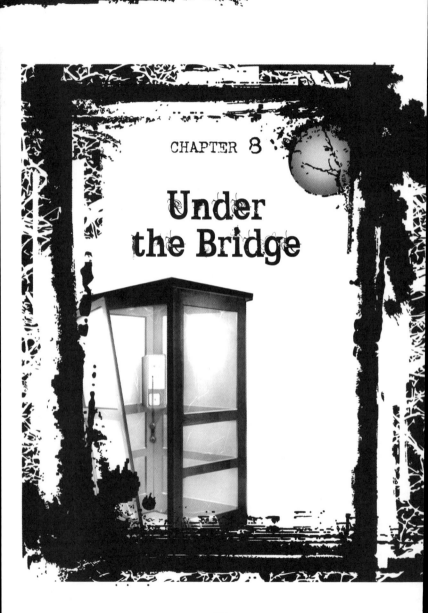

CHAPTER 8

Under the Bridge

The animal crossed the clearing in the direction of the bridge. Running, Janet caught up to it.

"Down there?" she said. "Lola is down there?" The dog vanished into the thick grass. Then it came back, barking loudly.

"Wait!" Janet called, pushing her way into the trees. "Just wait!"

Again the animal raced away, down a path that followed the slope. Janet stumbled along behind.

She tried to keep sight of the dog's tail without losing her footing, but the path was steep, and she stopped.

Only twenty feet from her was the bridge and, beneath it, the deep darkness.

"Patch," she called. "Patchy, stop. Stop, please." She raised her hands to her mouth, and called, "Lola? Lola? Are you there?"

Nothing.

She went on a few feet, but she was scared of falling into the darkness.

She stopped and called again. "Lola! If you're there, answer me! Answer me or come out! I hate this game. Lola!"

Nothing.

CHAPTER 9

A Whisper

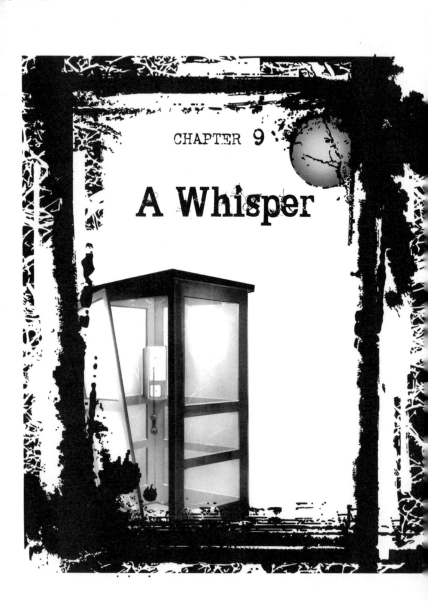

The animal did not stop.

Each time Janet called, it returned to her, but the dog clearly wanted Janet to follow it. So she did.

She kept following even when it was hard to keep going. Her feet caught on roots. She brushed against a patch of thorns, feeling their sting, but she did not stop. She could not.

If this was not a game, if Lola was there beneath the bridge, in trouble, in the darkness, if Lola was her friend, Janet had to find her.

When Janet reached the bridge she stood still, her hands again at her face.

Did she have to keep going? Did she have to go beneath, into the darkness?

She tried to be brave.

She whispered, "Lola? Lola?" She was hoping to hear any response.

Softly, from beneath the bridge, she heard, "Janet . . . Janet . . ."

It was no more than a whisper, the softest breath. She was certain of it. She was sure that she heard it. She peered into the dark.

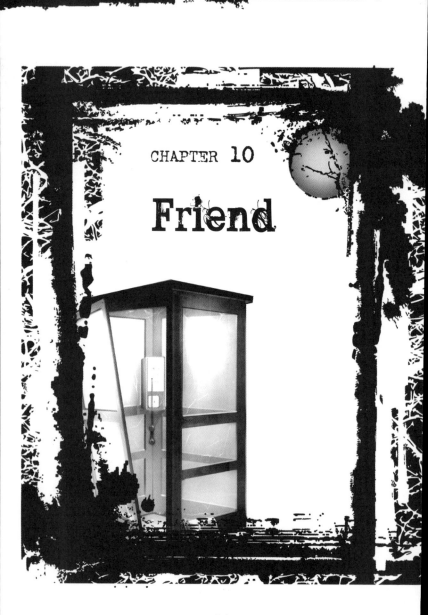

CHAPTER 10

Friend

At first, she couldn't see anything.

Then, by the silver bands of light falling from the gaps in the bridge above, Janet thought she saw Patch's eyes high up in the dark shadows, where the grass touched the bridge.

Also, there was a smell. It was a musty, old animal smell.

"Patch?" she said, then, "Lola?"

As she spoke, the eyes vanished and appeared again, higher, almost above her.

"Lola?" she begged.

Nothing.

Janet took a deep breath. "Lola, I'm sick of this. If this is a game, I hate it! Come out. Come out now."

The eyes narrowed, looking cruel.

"Lola," Janet cried, "if you don't come out now you're not my friend. You're like the other girls. You're tricking me. If you are, I don't care. I was all right by myself. I don't need you, or anyone. And anyway, I lost your stupid troll."

Out of the darkness, the white dog appeared.

It stood on its back legs, standing tall, as tall as Janet. Then it pranced in the darkness, stretching, growing, its form constantly changing into a new shape before Janet's face.

Human shape.

There, circling one eye, was the mark of the dog. The black patch.

"Patch?" Janet's lips could hardly move. "Lola?"

At the sound of the name, the eyes flickered and the patch grew, spreading, covering the white skin all over with hair, dark blue and shiny.

It smelled wet and musty.

Suddenly, Janet knew what was standing before her.

It wasn't a dog or a human. It was a beast. A huge, troll-shaped beast.

Janet screamed as the thing came closer and closer.

A word came out of the darkness and rang throughout the clearing.

The word rose and fell to fade and die far away in the woods.

"Friend," it echoed, "friend."

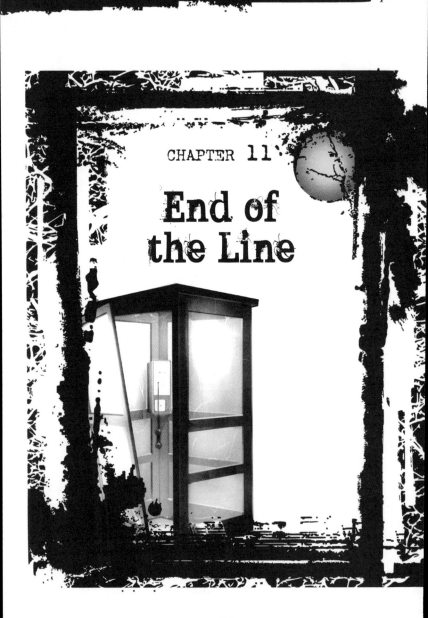

CHAPTER 11

End of
the Line

When the last bus clattered over the bridge and pulled into the stop, the driver leaned down to make sure no one was waiting. He would have been surprised if anyone was.

In all his years on the midnight run, no one had ever been waiting at the Half Moon stop. He had dropped off a few at the end of the line, but no one had ever gotten on the bus there.

There, on the ground outside the phone booth, was a bag. A duffel bag.

He opened the door of the bus and climbed out. He reached down and picked the bag up.

Inside the phone booth, he saw, was a book, its pages turning this way and that. He opened the door and lifted the book by its pages. He looked around again.

Nobody.

He put the book in the bag. But as he turned to go, a sudden movement caught his eye. He stood still, watching, and from the darkness behind the phone box came a dog. It was white, with a patch around one golden eye.

"Hello, Patchy," he said as the animal rolled at his feet. "Are you hanging around again? I haven't seen you for a while. Don't you have a home to go to?"

As the driver stooped to pat the dog's stomach, he saw something in the dirt. He picked it up and turned it in his fingers.

It was some kind of monster doll, a troll thing, with a silver chain dangling from its head of dark blue hair. The driver turned and tossed it away over the bridge.

The dog saw. It jumped up, racing after it into the deepest darkness beneath the Half Moon Bridge.

ABOUT THE AUTHOR

Gary Crew has been writing books for young people since 1985, when he was a high school teacher. He has won numerous awards for his science fiction and mystery titles. He currently lives in the mountains of eastern Australia with his wife, Christine, and his dogs, Ferris, Beulah, and Miss Wendy.

ABOUT THE ILLUSTRATOR

Gregory Rogers lives in Brisbane, Australia. He studied fine art and worked as a graphic designer before he began illustrating books. In 1995, Gregory became the first Australian illustrator to win the prestigious Kate Greenaway medal. In his spare time, he loves playing music. He also collects CDs, antiques, books, and anything that might get dusty.

GLOSSARY

awkward (AWK-wurd)—not able to relax and talk to people easily

bracelet (BRAYSS-lit)—jewelry worn around the wrist

clearing (KLEER-ing)—an area in a forest or woods where no trees grow, or where the trees have been removed

cruel (KROO-uhl)—being mean or causing pain to someone on purpose

donations (doh-NAY-shuhnz)—money given to help others

lever (LEV-ur)—a bar or a handle that you use to work or control a machine

spine (SPYN)—the backbone of an animal

troll (TROHL)—in fairy tales, a creature that lives under a bridge, in a cave, or in the hills

DISCUSSION QUESTIONS

1. Why are the other girls cruel to Janet? Why isn't Lola cruel to her?

2. Lola thought she would prove her friendship to Janet by stealing a keychain for her. What do you think about that? Is that a good way to show friendship, or are there better ways? What are some ways to show your friendship?

3. Why do you think Lola gave Janet a troll keychain? What do trolls symbolize?

4. At the end of the story, Janet sees the strange thing coming out of the darkness. The thing says, "Friend." Who, or what, is that thing? Where is Lola?

WRITING PROMPTS

1. In chapter 10, Janet meets the strange, hairy creature. We never see what happens next. Write another chapter that explains what happened to Janet and Lola.

2. Janet finds herself all alone at a strange bus stop in the middle of nowhere. What would you do in her situation?

3. Sometimes it can be interesting to think about a story from a different point of view. Try writing chapter 2 from Lola's point of view. What does she think of her new school and the people in it? What does she like about it and dislike?

TAKE A DEEP BREATH AND

TRAPPED

BY JAMES MOLONEY

STONE ARCH *Fantasy*

David's new town is boring until he discovers a big drainpipe that looks perfect for skateboarding. He can't resist exploring the huge cement tunnel. Then he hears something odd. Someone else is inside the tunnel, in the darkness, where no living person should be.

STEP INTO THE SHADE!

THE PLAGUE

BY JONATHAN HARLEN

STONE ARCH *Fantasy*

Melissa and Will just wanted to go into the pet store and take a quick look at the exotic pets. Without warning, the store's sick owner, Mr. Brinkley, bites Will on his arm! Hours later, Will becomes sick too. Do the animals carry a dangerous plague?

INTERNET SITES

Do you want to know more about subjects related to this book? Or are you interested in learning about other topics? Then check out FactHound, a fun, easy way to find Internet sites.

Our investigative staff has already sniffed out great sites for you!

Here's how to use FactHound:

1. Visit *www.facthound.com*

2. Select your grade level.

3. To learn more about subjects related to this book, type in the book's ISBN number: **1598898590**.

4. Click the **Fetch It** button.

FactHound will fetch the best Internet sites for you!